DIA
ICE P

On Thin Ice

For Eoin, Leonora, and Beatrice

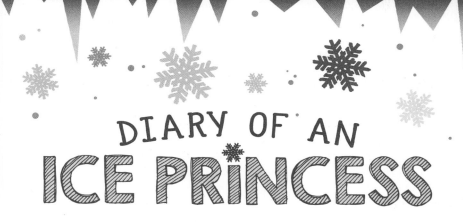

DIARY OF AN
ICE PRINCESS

On Thin Ice

Christina Soontornvat

Illustrations by
Barbara Szepesi Szucs

SCHOLASTIC INC.

THE TRUTH ABOUT FIELD TRIPS

✳ FRIDAY ✳

Diary, I am so excited!

Next week our class is going to do something called a *field trip*. When our teacher, Ms. Collier, first talked about it, I thought she meant we would take a trip to a field. We don't have fields up here in the clouds, so I thought it sounded fun.

I was even more excited when my best friend, Claudia, explained things.

"A field trip is when you get to go

somewhere outside school," she said. "We all pack bag lunches, and the school bus will pick us up and take us somewhere cool."

I gasped with excitement. "Like the post office?"

Claudia laughed. "Even cooler than that. This year, our class is visiting Oceanside Aquarium."

An aquarium! I love animals that live underwater, even though I haven't had much luck with taking care of them at home. Diary, I'm sure you remember the disaster that happened when I tried to set up an aquarium in my room.

Luckily, we hadn't bought any fish yet.
That was back when my winter magic
used to slip out without my control.
I know for sure nothing like that will
happen again.

This field trip is going to be so cool.
I wish we could go tomorrow. But

WANTED TO TALK TO YOU ABOUT. DID YOU KNOW THAT LITTLE JACK IS COMING UP FOR A VISIT FROM THE SOUTHERN HEMISPHERE?"

A half-sad, half-happy look flashed on Mom's face. "Is he really? We haven't seen him in years."

My cousin Jack lives with my great-Aunt Sunder way down at the bottom of the globe, near Antarctica. My great-Aunt Sunder is Granddad's sister, but she never comes to our family gatherings. I don't think they get along.

"HE WAS SUPPOSED TO STAY WITH ME," said Granddad. **"BUT PERHAPS HE COULD STAY WITH YOU INSTEAD.**

GRANDDAD

GREAT-AUNT SUNDER

GREAT-AUNT EASTIA

GREAT-UNCLE WESTON

HE COULD GIVE LINA SOME LESSONS, WINTERHEART TO WINTERHEART."

Before I had even two seconds to think about it, Mom piped up. "That's a great idea, Dad. We'd love to have him stay with us."

Diary, this family never asks me what I think about anything.

3

BEWARE OF COUSINS

Tonight after dinner I called Claudia to tell her about my cousin's visit.

Claudia is the only one at school who knows about my family's magic powers. Luckily, she's great at keeping secrets.

"Your cousin is Jack *Frost*?" Claudia exclaimed. "That's so wild."

"It's no wilder than my grandfather being the North Wind."

"I guess not. But isn't Jack Frost like a little elf who goes around putting snowflakes on windowpanes?"

"He's not an elf, but according to Granddad, he's really good at winter magic. Some people even call him the Prince of Winter."

The only memory I have of my cousin Jack is from a family reunion at Granddad's castle when Jack froze my diaper.

My family still loves to remind me about that story. So embarrassing.

"I know he's a Winterheart like me," I explained. "But other than that I don't know much about him."

"Well, I hope you hid your diary and put a lock on your bedroom door," said Claudia.

"Wait, why?" I asked.

"Because cousins are trouble. Trust me, I have four cousins my age and all of them are pests. They'll annoy you just like brothers, but it's worse because your parents won't discipline them."

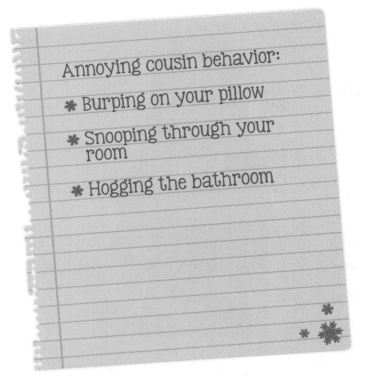

Annoying cousin behavior:

* Burping on your pillow
* Snooping through your room
* Hogging the bathroom

"How long is he supposed to stay with you?"

I gulped. "The whole week."

Claudia let out a whistle. "It's been nice knowing you."

Diary, do you think Claudia is right? I don't want an obnoxious pest staying with us, even if he is the Prince of Winter!

4

ICE TO MEET YOU

※ SUNDAY ※

Cousin Jack arrived after dinner.

Mom and I were playing cards in the front room when we heard the *zhoom!* of Dad's airplane engine. Dad's a pilot, and he had zipped over to Granddad's castle to pick Jack up and give him a ride.

※ 19 ※

Gusty and I hurried to the window.
Even though I dreaded all the things
Claudia told me, I was really curious too.

So imagine my surprise when my
mom opened the door and in walked
Cousin Jack:

PLEASANT SMILE

BIG BOUQUET OF FLOWERS

DAPPER SUIT

Jack bowed to Mom and handed her the bouquet. "Hello, Aunt Gale. It's so nice to see you again. Thank you for having me in your home."

"Are these snowbells? Jack, they are just lovely!" said Mom.

Then Jack bowed to me. "It's nice to

see you again, Cousin Lina. I'm looking forward to spending time with you."

Diary, my mouth had fallen open and I had to remind myself to close it! A suit? Flowers? Suddenly I felt really awkward in my own castle. Like he was the prince and I was a visiting nobody.

Mom said, "Lina, why don't you show Jack up to his room? I'm sure he's tired from his flight."

As we started upstairs, Gusty came bounding over. He leaped up off the ground and jumped into Jack's arms. I was surprised because normally Gusty only does that for me.

Jack laughed as Gusty licked his face. "Ha-ha, Lina, your dog is really sweet!"

Well, Diary, anyone who loves Gusty has got to be okay. So at least he was starting off on the right foot.

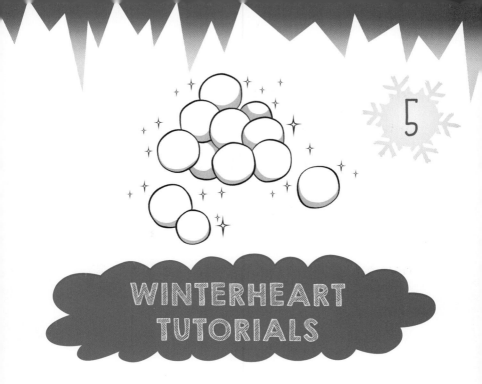

5

WINTERHEART TUTORIALS

I showed Cousin Jack to the guest room down the hall from me.

"There's breakfast in the morning downstairs," I explained. "On the weekends my dad makes pancakes."

Jack nodded. "Shaped like clouds, right?"

"You remember that?"

Jack smiled. "I don't remember much, but I definitely remember those pancakes. And I remember Granddad singing, *'Fly me to the moon . . .'*"

"You mean, *'FLY ME TO THE MOON . . .'* Granddad yells even when he sings."

"And . . ." Jack got a funny look on his face and smiled. ". . . I remember when your diaper froze. You ran around the room screaming, 'Butt cold! Butt cold!'"

I burst out laughing. "I did not!"

"You totally did!"

I crossed my arms. "Well, that was

mean of you to freeze my diaper."

"I didn't do it! I got in trouble for it, but it wasn't my fault. I think you froze it yourself, but that was back when no one knew that you were a Winterheart."

"Oh, right. I didn't figure my powers out until a few months ago," I said. "Before that I was always messing things up with snow and ice."

"That's why I'm here, right?" said Jack. "To help you learn to control your powers even better."

"Granddad says you're really good at winter magic."

I didn't say the other thing I was

thinking: *And I'm not nearly as good as you are.*

Jack straightened his suit and smiled. "I guess I'm okay at it."

6

PUTTING ON A SNOW

Diary, when it comes to winter magic,
Cousin Jack is not just okay.

He's *incredible*.

We all sat at the table after dinner
while he showed us some of the things
he could do.

Jack's magic is so different from

mine. Everything he made was so delicate and pretty. I never even knew that winter magic could look like that.

"You have to use the nature of snow and ice to your advantage," Jack explained. "Every snowflake has its own crystal pattern. No two snowflakes are alike."

Of course I know that already, Diary. It's not like I was born snowing yesterday. But I didn't say anything.

Jack leaned toward the vase of snowbells and pointed to one of the blossoms. "Focus your magic on just one snowflake, and allow your magic to flow out from there, building and building, crystal by crystal."

Jack held his finger over a flower. Suddenly a tiny fleck of frost appeared on the petal. The frost spread slowly over the snowbell until the entire blossom was covered in delicate, icy lace.

"You try," Jack said to me.

I leaned forward. *A single snowflake,* I told myself.

A pattern of frost formed on one of the flowers. That wasn't so hard! But then I felt the ice crystals getting out of control. The pretty frost thickened, and in no time the entire bouquet of snowbells was encased in a thick cocoon of solid ice.

"Don't get discouraged, Lina," said Jack. "When you're just starting out, it's natural to make simple mistakes."

I'm not *just* starting out, Diary! I've been using Winterheart magic for months now.

"I know how to make frost," I said. "It just got a little away from me this time, that's all."

"Lina, no need to get upset," said Mom.

"I'm not upset," I said, trying to make my voice as un-upset as possible. "I'm just distracted because I have a lot of homework."

"What's your homework?" asked Jack.

I didn't mean to sound annoyed, Diary, but I guess I was. "It's nothing. Just something for school."

"About that, Lina," said Mom. "Your

dad and I were thinking that it would be good for Jack to go to school with you this week. I've talked to the principal and she said he could be a visiting student." She smiled at Jack. "Of course you'll have to keep your powers a secret."

"Oh, that's no problem, Aunt Gale," said Jack. "I've got my magic completely under control."

Diary, I know this is weird, but I wish Jack was the burp-on-your-pillow sort of cousin. It turns out the perfect-in-every-way sort is even more annoying.

7

THE PRINCE OF PERFECT

☀ MONDAY ☀

This morning Dad dropped us off near
the school in the plane, and Jack and I
walked together to the front door.
I could tell that Jack was nervous.

"Is my hair sticking up in the back?"
he asked.

"For the thousandth time, no," I said with a laugh. "Relax. School's not nearly as scary as you think it will be."

To be fair, I remember how it felt walking into a Groundling school for the first time. But at least I knew

Claudia on my first day. She was a
school expert. Jack didn't know anyone
but me. I have to admit that I liked the
feeling of having him depend on me.

It didn't last too long, though.

"Class, I want you all to welcome
Lina's cousin, Jack," said Ms. Collier.
"Jack is a visiting student from . . .
Where did you say you were from
again, dear?"

All of Jack's nervousness seemed to
melt away. "I live near Antarctica, ma'am."

The whole class murmured oohs
and aahs.

"It's a cool place to live. Like, literally
it gets down to negative seventy-five

degrees," said Jack. Everyone laughed.
"But it's really beautiful too. There are
places where the ice glows blue. And of
course there's my penguins."

"*Your* penguins?" asked Claudia. "Like
they're your pets?"

Jack flashed a smile. "No, not pets. But I call them mine because the same colony comes back to the same spot every year. You should see the babies. They're like tiny balls of fluff."

"Aw, that sounds so cute!" said Claudia. Everyone sighed dreamily.

"Penguins are one of the animals we'll see on our field trip," said Ms. Collier. "All week we'll be working on projects to learn how animals are adapted to their environments."

"I'd be happy to give a special presentation on penguins and their adaptations to the cold," said Jack.

Claudia tapped me on the shoulder. "Wow, I was totally wrong," she whispered. "Your cousin isn't bad at all. He's like the perfect kid."

I had to agree. Diary, is there such a thing as being too perfect?

8

OH MY ORANGES

At lunch I was hoping that I'd get a break from my cousin and take some time to just hang out with Claudia.

No such luck.

Jack sat down on the other side of her, and soon they were talking all about

penguins. Claudia loves penguins, so they had a lot to talk about.

"The male emperor penguins take care of the eggs while they wait for the females to return," said Jack.

"Isn't it amazing?" said Claudia. "They

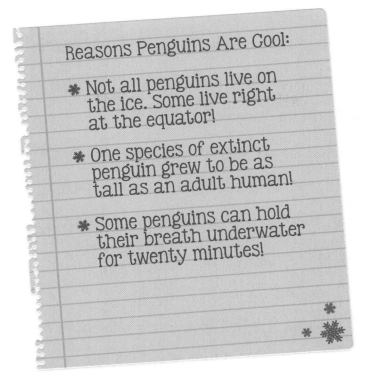

Reasons Penguins Are Cool:

* Not all penguins live on the ice. Some live right at the equator!

* One species of extinct penguin grew to be as tall as an adult human!

* Some penguins can hold their breath underwater for twenty minutes!

don't eat for four whole months until she gets back!"

Jack went to get some more ketchup. While he was gone, I took the opportunity to have a heart-to-heart with my best friend.

"Hey, can I talk to you?" I whispered.
"Don't you think that Jack is showing
off a little too much?"

Claudia shrugged. "At least he doesn't
hide your stuff or put his boogers on
your toothbrush. I think he's just trying
to make a good impression."

I sighed. "I know . . ."

"Listen, Lina, I know it's probably not
easy having someone like Jack living with
you. He's so good at everything. I'd be
jealous of him too."

"Jealous?" I gasped. "I am not jealous
of him!"

Before I could argue with her,
Jack came strolling back to the table

with a tray full of paper cups.

"Hey, guys, look what I found." The
paper cups were filled with orange
wedges from the cafeteria. They were
frosted over, like icy orange pops.

Jack handed the frosty orange
treats around to all my friends at the

table. He must have made them with winter magic! Using our magic powers at school was definitely not allowed. But what Jack had done was so subtle, no one would be able to tell it was magic and not just refrigeration.

"Ooh, this is so yummy!" said one kid.

"Yeah, where did you get these?" asked another.

"Who cares—they're delicious!" said another boy. "Three cheers for Jack!"

Jack smiled and handed me an orange slice.

Diary, it tasted as sour as a lemon in my mouth.

THE LONGEST WEEK

☀ WEDNESDAY ☀

I don't know how it happened, Diary,
but my cousin Jack has become the
most popular kid in the entire school.
Even the fifth graders stop by the
playground at recess to give him high
fives and ask about his adventures

tracking leopard seals off the coast of
Australia.

It's irritating. But the most irritating
thing is that I couldn't stop thinking
about how Claudia called me jealous. I'm
not jealous. I just don't like the way Jack

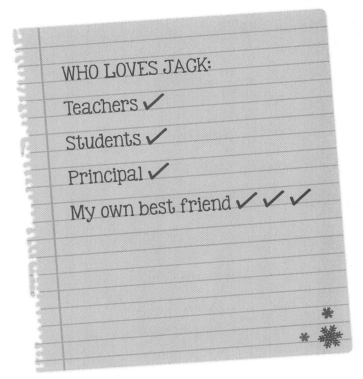

WHO LOVES JACK:
Teachers ✔
Students ✔
Principal ✔
My own best friend ✔ ✔ ✔

tries to show off when other people are around. He doesn't act like that when we're by ourselves.

"Hey, Lina," said Mom when I walked into her office. "Long day at school, huh?"

"The longest."

"Well, I was thinking that the three of us could make pizza together and play some games afterward."

I perked up. "Yes, I'd love to do that with you and Dad!"

"Oh no, sweetie, your dad is going to be home late. I meant you, me, and Jack."

I didn't respond, but my mom never misses a thing. "What's going on? Is he being mean to you?"

"No," I grumbled. "Of course not. Mr. Perfect would never be mean to anyone."

"Ah, I see. Honey, it's perfectly normal to feel a little—"

"Do not tell me I'm jealous! I am *not* jealous. I just want a little space from him, that's all."

Mom nodded. "I understand. It's not easy having someone live with you twenty-four seven. But sweetheart, please don't be hard on your cousin. He really looks up to you, and he needs you to be there for him."

Looks up to me? Needs me? Are you kidding, Diary? Jack thinks he's better than me at everything! We need each other like we need frostbite.

But I wasn't going to say that out loud. It would only make Jack seem more perfect than me.

I trudged upstairs to my room, ready to chill out with Gusty. As I passed the guest room, I peeked in and saw Gusty snuggling on Jack's lap, getting an ear scratch.

Diary, even my own dog likes my cousin more than me!

A JAR FULL OF PERFECTION

Even though Jack is driving me a little bonkers, nothing can ruin Ms. Collier's class for me.

"All right, young naturalists, let's get ready to go outside!"

Ms. Collier has been calling us

"naturalists" this week, which is someone who studies the natural world.

"When we go to the aquarium, we'll be observing all sorts of interesting living things," said Ms. Collier. "But we can't forget that we have nature all around us, even in the schoolyard."

Our assignment was to go outside and collect specimens that we could bring back to the classroom to talk about their adaptations. Some kids were going to gather plants. Others were going to sketch birds that fly over the school.

Claudia and I decided to look for insects.

Outside, it turned out to be harder to

gather insects than we thought. The
ants bit us. We couldn't find any beetles.
The flies and grasshoppers were too
fast. I looked around the schoolyard.
Jack was standing near the other kids,
holding his jar up.

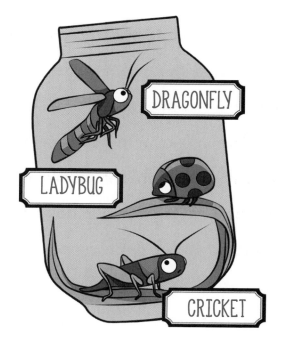

How in the world did he collect so many? I watched him and realized he was using his frost magic to stun the insects. That made them slow enough to catch in his jar. As soon as the insects warmed up, they were flying around again, totally fine.

If Jack could do that, so could I.

I searched the ground until I found a perfect specimen: a spider.

Yes, Diary, I know. Spiders are not insects. They are arachnids. But hey, I needed *something* for our adaptation project, and the spider was perfect.

I carefully waved my finger over the spider, doing exactly what Jack had

taught me: freezing the air, crystal by

crystal.

"Just a little cold . . ." I whispered.

But I must have slipped up, because

all of a sudden a ball of snow formed

above the spider and dumped right on

top of him.

"Oh no, oh no!" I gasped.

Jack and Claudia came running over. We scooped up the snowball and set it in the sun.

While we waited for it to melt, my heart was racing. What if my magic killed the spider? I'd feel so terrible!

But luckily, as soon as the snow melted, the spider seemed just fine.

Arachnids are tough little creatures, Diary.

We decided not to put it in the jar. The poor thing had been through enough. Ms. Collier called, and the three of us started walking back to the school building.

Claudia put her hand on my shoulder. I think she knew I felt bad about the spider. "Don't worry, maybe Jack can give us one of his specimens to do the project with."

Jack held up his jar full of insects. "I've got more than enough to share. And hey, Lina . . ." He lowered his voice. "I think you probably shouldn't use your winter magic at school anymore."

"But *you* did!" Of course I know I am definitely not supposed to do magic on the ground. But it was so unfair that Jack got to and I didn't.

"That's different," said Jack. "I can use my magic in a really small and controlled way. Until you learn to do it like me, maybe it's better if you just hold off."

Diary, even though my magic is all about the cold, in that moment I was boiling mad.

COUSIN MYSTERIES

Diary, there are many unexplained

mysteries of the universe:

* Where do giant squid go to have babies?

* Why do narwhals have horns?

* What's up with my cousin Jack?

I'm serious, Diary, I cannot figure him out. After his comment in the schoolyard, I was ready to come home and avoid him. But as soon as we got up to the palace, he wanted to play.

We went out to the castle gardens and made an icy obstacle course. It had three sections.

1. Surf down the frozen ice wave.

2. Walk across the wobbly ice beam on your tiptoes.

3. Leap over the snow barrels, through the icy ring!

We were actually having a really good time! Jack was acting completely normal and not showing off at all. But then my dad came outside, and Jack just had to impress him by making a toy ice plane, complete with a tiny ice propeller.

"And the thing actually flies?" said
Dad. "Wow, Lina, did you see this? It's
incredible!"

I don't get it. If Jack knows he's so
much better than me, why does he
always want to hang around me? I can't
figure out if he wants to be my friend,
or if he just wants someone to show off
in front of. Is this how all cousins are?

As for learning how to do subtle
winter magic, I haven't made any
progress. Maybe I could learn if I
had a different teacher. But when
Jack's around, all I can think about is
how I'll never be as good as he is.

Things are pretty confusing these

days, Diary. But one thing I know for sure is that tomorrow is our field trip to the aquarium, and nothing in the world is going to ruin it for me.

THE WHEELS ON THE BUS ARE TOTALLY AWESOME

✳ FRIDAY ✳

When I first learned that I would get to attend Hilltop Science and Arts Academy, there was one thing I was most excited about: riding on a school bus.

What I love about the bus:

＊ So yellow

＊ So shiny

＊ So . . . bus-like

Sadly, none of the Hilltop bus routes go up into the sky, so I was stuck riding to school in Dad's airplane.

But all of that changed today. Today I boarded a school bus for the first time ever! Claudia and I sat next to each other, of course.

As the bus took off, I felt a little thrill in my stomach. I have hardly ever ridden in a car, much less a giant school bus!

Hilltop Academy is only a few miles from the ocean, and soon the bus was driving along the coast road. I could look out the window and see the water stretching out to the sky.

Claudia tugged my sleeve. "Hey, what's wrong with your cousin? Is he sick?"

Jack stared out the window in the other direction. He had been really quiet that morning.

I shrugged. "Who knows. He's probably thinking up new winter magic lessons for me."

"How much longer is he staying with you?" asked Claudia.

"Granddad is picking him up this weekend to take him back down south." (Which isn't soon enough, in my opinion.)

The bus pulled up to a long pier that jutted out into the ocean. The Oceanside Aquarium was built right on the pier. So cool!

The aquarium manager was there to greet us.

"Welcome, Ms. Collier's class!" she said. "Today we are going to start off with an introduction to all the different underwater habitats we have here at the aquarium. Afterward, we've got a fun scavenger hunt that will get you thinking all about animal adaptations. The first team to complete the scavenger hunt will get a special prize!"

As soon as the introductory tour was finished, Ms. Collier split us into teams of three for the scavenger hunt. Claudia, Jack, and I were on a team.

"Come on, let's get started!" said Jack.

I followed him and Claudia, wondering which version of Jack he'd be today: the cool cousin version, or the show-off version.

13

SHOW-OFF
SNOW-OFF

Our team blazed through the scavenger

hunt questions:

QUESTION: Find an animal that cleans
            for its dinner.
ANSWER: Cleaner shrimp remove
          parasites from fish. The fish
          stays healthy, and the shrimp
          gets a meal!

QUESTION: Find an animal with two eyes trained on the surface.
ANSWER: Flounder fish spend their lives hiding on the seafloor. They have both eyes on one side of their body so they can see predators lurking above!

Diary, life has been on earth for almost four billion years. That means there are a ton of incredible adaptations to observe!

It was almost time to head back to Ms. Collier, but we still had one more adaptation on our list to find:

QUESTION: Find an animal that uses its wings to fly through the sea.

What could it be? A flying fish? A stingray?

"I know," said Claudia. "It has to be penguins! Their wings are useless for flying through the air, but they can soar underwater."

"To the penguin exhibit!" said Jack.

The penguins were on the bottom floor of the aquarium in a huge enclosure that was kept chilly so they'd be comfortable. A deep tank of cold water separated the penguins from the visitors.

The aquarium manager was coming out of the exhibit as we were going in.

"Great timing," said the manager, holding the door for us. "I've just fed them, so they should be really active."

"Oh my glaciers, look at them!" I said. The penguins were so cute, waddling across the ice and then sliding on their bellies into the water.

"We have to find the species name for our scavenger hunt," said Claudia, searching for a label.

"These are chinstrap penguins," said Jack. He added, "There are about twenty species of penguins in the world, and I can name them all." He touched the glass with his finger, and the word *chinstrap* appeared in swirly frosted letters.

Even now, when it was only the three of us, Jack just had to be a show-off.

Well, Diary, I was tired of letting him get away with it. I double-checked to make sure no one else was in the exhibit hall with us. "If we're going to use our magic down here, maybe we should do something more practical."

I raised my hands and curled my fingers in a circle. A spiraling slide of ice formed on the penguin habitat. The penguins waddled up to the top and slid down on their bellies, around and around.

Claudia laughed. "Oh my gosh, they love that!"

"Not bad . . ." said Jack slowly. "But it could use some flair, don't you think?" He waved his fingers at the glass, and formed a slide of his own with fancy curlicue decorations made out of spindly ice crystals.

I frowned. With a wave of my hand, I made snow fall inside the exhibit. I used my powers to scoop the snow into a ramp that the penguins could use to launch themselves into the water.

Jack made his own ramp, with fancy fish decorations etched onto the side.

"Okay, guys, I think you can stop now . . ." said Claudia.

But we couldn't stop. We kept going, using our powers to create bigger and better additions to the penguin exhibit. The penguins loved it. They were sliding and flipping and jumping all over the place on the icy playground we were building for them.

"Hey, it's getting really cold in here," said Claudia, shivering. "You should probably cut it out now."

But every time I made something, Jack had to make it better. When I built an ice structure, he had to make one fancier and prettier than mine. If he

wouldn't stop, then neither would I.

Finally, Claudia stepped in between Jack and me. "You guys, I said that's *enough!*"

Claudia was right. It was more than enough.

Diary, I couldn't hold my feelings inside for one more second.

14

A WINTER HEART-TO-HEART

"WHY DO YOU ALWAYS HAVE TO SHOW OFF THAT YOU'RE BETTER THAN ME?" I shouted. (I am the granddaughter of the North Wind, after all.)

Jack looked shocked. "What are you talking about?"

"You have to be better than me at everything. Frost magic. Collecting specimens. Making friends. Even making penguin playgrounds!"

"Lina, I didn't mean to make you so mad."

"You didn't make me mad, you made me . . ."

(Oh, Diary, I really hate it when Claudia's right about things like this.)

". . . you made me feel jealous of you. And it's not cool!"

"*You're* jealous of *me*?" Jack's eyes were wide. "But Lina, I'm the one who should be jealous of *you*."

I did a double take. Make that a
triple take.

Jack took a deep breath. "You have
everything. A nice mom and dad, an
awesome home, a great best friend. I
don't have any of that down south. It's

just me and Great-Aunt Sunder, and she's not the friendliest person to be around. I'd way rather have what you've got."

Could that be true, Diary? Could Jack Frost, the Prince of Winter, be jealous of me?

"But you're way better at winter magic than me," I said.

"I'm not better. I'm just different. Look at all the creative stuff you made. I just copied you and made it fancy."

I crossed my arms. That was definitely true.

Jack let out a sigh. "I'm really sorry for showing off all the time. I wasn't trying to make you feel bad. I just thought that if everyone saw I was so good at winter magic, they'd ask me to come back and teach you again."

I thought about some things I'd noticed earlier in the week:

* Mom said Jack looks up to me and needs my support.

* Jack stares out the window really sad sometimes.

* Jack always wants to be around me, even when we aren't getting along.

I realized that when Jack goes home, he won't have a school to go back to. He'll be all alone again. Diary, a part of me really wanted to stay mad at him. But another part of me understood exactly what it feels like to be super lonely.

Since Jack had apologized, I decided I would give him a second chance.

I uncrossed my arms. "I do want you to come back and stay with us."

Now Jack did the triple take. "Seriously?"

I held up one finger. "With some conditions."

Jack nodded.

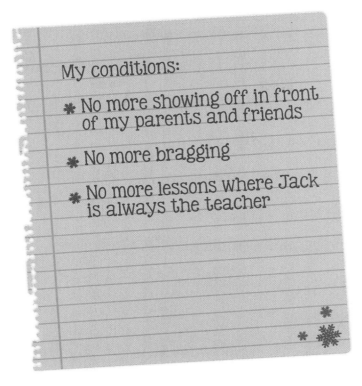

My conditions:

❄ No more showing off in front of my parents and friends

❄ No more bragging

❄ No more lessons where Jack is always the teacher

"There's lots of stuff I know how to do that you don't," I said. "We can learn from each other."

"I like that one," said Claudia.

Jack raised his hand like he was

taking an oath. "You're totally right. And I promise that if I ever show off again, you can dump a whole cloud's worth of snow on my head."

I laughed. We shook hands to seal the deal.

Claudia applauded. "It's just like I always told you, Lina. Cousins are the best."

Our laughter was cut short by the aquarium manager running into the exhibit.

"We have an emergency," she said. "The temperature in the aquarium is dropping to dangerous levels!"

We all looked around. Jack and I had

been so absorbed in our snowy

showdown that we hadn't noticed we'd

let our magic get out of hand.

The entire exhibit hall was coated

over in a thick layer of ice!

15

TOO COLD TO HANDLE

The manager stared in shock at the iced-over penguin habitat. "It looks like our temperature problem is coming from this exhibit hall. The penguins will be fine, but a lot of our animals aren't adapted to live in cold water. If we don't raise the temperature soon, they could be in real trouble."

Diary, it was all our fault!

Jack and I had been so busy competing with each other that we had gone overboard with our magic. In the penguin exhibit, little icebergs floated on

top of the slushy seawater. We'd made it way too cold in there.

"We need to raise the temperature fast," said the manager. "But I can't find my key that unlocks the thermostat. I must have dropped it here somewhere."

We all helped her search the floor and under the seats, but we didn't see the key anywhere. Finally, Claudia tapped my shoulder and pointed at the penguin tank.

A tiny brass key lay on the very bottom of the pool. The manager probably dropped it when she was feeding the penguins.

But how to get it out?

The water was deep and almost freezing. The penguins loved it, but they had thick blubber and feathers that kept them insulated. If a human was going to get that key, they'd need a wet suit and a scuba tank.

We didn't have enough time for that.

Jack had just told me that I'm creative with my winter magic.
I needed to be super creative, and I needed to hurry.

I watched the penguins dive around the ice floating at the top of the water.

That was it!

I whispered my idea to Jack.

He grinned. "Lina, that's brilliant!"

"Do you want to do the magic?" I asked him.

I waited to see if he'd jump in and take over, but he shook his head. "You've got this, Cousin."

I smiled. I guess Jack really had learned something.

Now the question was: Had I?

16

CRYSTAL BY CRYSTAL

"You distract the manager," I whispered to Claudia.

Claudia nodded and led the manager away from the penguin tank.

I pushed up my sleeves and held my arms toward the key at the bottom of the pool. I needed to concentrate. I couldn't let my magic get out of hand, or else the entire pool of water would freeze. Then we'd never get the key out.

"You can do it, Lina," whispered Jack.

I took a deep breath. I needed to think small and subtle. One ice crystal at a time.

I shut one eye and wiggled my pinkie finger at the key. Crystal by crystal, I built a tiny sphere of ice around the key. As soon as the ice ball hardened, I pulled my hand back. I opened both eyes.

The ice didn't spread. I had done it! Small and subtle.

Ice is less dense than liquid water, so

you can guess what happened next,
Diary.

It floated straight to the top!

"Ma'am!" I called to the aquarium
manager. "Is that your key? Floating
there on the water?"

The manager gasped in surprise. "But how in the world . . ." Then she looked up at the icy slides and ramps Jack and I had made. "Wow, I'm going to need to give our exhibits designer a raise."

The manager broke the key out of the ice bubble, and we all rushed with her to the master thermostat. She unlocked the box and dialed up the temperature just in time. All the animals were fine. Thank goodness. I would have felt terrible if even one little cleaner shrimp got hurt because of me.

Outside, we joined Ms. Collier and the rest of the class by the bus.

"Where have you three been?" she asked us.

"Lina and Claudia were busy saving the aquarium," said Jack. "They were amazing."

Then he took a step back while the whole class clapped and cheered.

Diary, that was pretty awesome, and not just because it happened in front of a school bus.

GOOD-BYE FOR NOW

* SATURDAY *

Today was equal parts happy and sad,
Diary.

It was Jack's last day staying with us.

If I had known that my cousin would
turn out to be so cool, I would have
spent the last week differently. But this

morning we made up for all the time we wasted competing with each other. We made our own ice slides and raced each other down them. Why should penguins get to have all the fun, right?

By the time Granddad came to pick Jack up, our cheeks were rosy and our ribs ached from laughing so hard.

"SO I TAKE IT THAT THE LESSONS WENT WELL, THEN, LINA?" he boomed.

"Actually, Lina is the one who taught me so many things," said Jack. "We're both definitely better at Winterheart magic now."

I smiled. Then I made my face get really serious. "Oh, but we have so much more to cover. Right, Jack? We'll have to have about a hundred more lessons, I think."

My mom put her hands on each of our shoulders. "We'll have to have Jack come stay with us again very soon, then."

Jack beamed. "I'd love that, Aunt Gale." He didn't do any formal bowing, but wrapped his arms around my mom and dad and gave them big hugs. Then Gusty jumped into his arms for a slobbery farewell. My dog is a great judge of character.

Then it was our turn to say good-bye.

"I'll write you a letter," said Jack.

"I'll write you one first."

We hugged each other. It's funny, but two kids with ice powers can give really warm hugs.

We stood out front and waved good-bye as my granddad lifted Jack up with his wind powers and blustered away, off to the Southern Hemisphere.

I was really sad, Diary. But I know I'm going to see him again.

Us Winterhearts have to stick together.

Blubber Up

Experiment with an animal adaptation
for living in icy cold water!

YOU WILL NEED:

* A large bowl filled with cold water
* Ice cubes
* Vegetable shortening, such as Crisco

STAYING WARM IS COOL

How do animals like penguins and polar bears tolerate living in the coldest environments on earth? Warm-blooded animals that make their homes in the polar seas must keep their body temperature constant to survive.

One adaptation they have that allows them to do this is *blubber*. Blubber is a thick layer of fat that surrounds the animal's body. Fatty tissue prevents heat from traveling through it, which helps *insulate*, or stop the animal's body heat from escaping into the cold water.

TRY IT OUT:

Let's see how well fat can insulate against the cold. Put ice cubes into the bowl of water and stir until the water gets really cold. Remove enough ice cubes so you will have room to place your fingers in the water without touching the ice.

Completely coat one of your fingers in a thick layer of vegetable shortening. Make sure you don't miss a spot!

Now submerge your shortening-coated finger and one uncoated finger in the bowl of ice water. Do you feel a difference? How long can you hold your fingers in the water before it's too cold to handle? Did your insulated finger last longer?

Vegetable shortening is a fat derived from plants. It doesn't insulate as well as blubber, but in this experiment it helps stop your body heat from escaping into the ice water.

Now go warm up—brr!

Be cool—not warm—and read a sneak peek of Lina's next adventure!

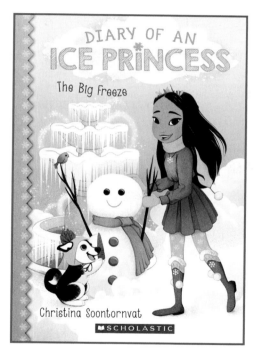

DIARY OF AN
ICE PRINCESS
The Big Freeze

Christina Soontornvat

■SCHOLASTIC

THE ART OF SURPRISE

* FRIDAY *

Dear Diary,

I've said this before, but I'll say it again: There is nothing I love more than school.

Except my family.

And my dog, Gusty.

Okay, and maybe my best friend, Claudia.

Okay, and maybe mango-and-whipped-cloud pudding—but you get the picture!

If the kids at school knew about my real life—that I'm a princess with magical winter powers who lives in a palace in the clouds—they'd probably wish we could trade places. But I just love knowing that when I walk through the doors of Hilltop Science and Arts Academy, something exciting is going to happen.

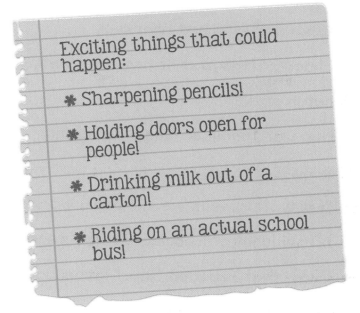

Exciting things that could happen:

* Sharpening pencils!

* Holding doors open for people!

* Drinking milk out of a carton!

* Riding on an actual school bus!

Of course the best thing about school is science class. Our teacher, Ms. Collier, comes up with the coolest experiments. Which is why I was so happy this morning to hear her say, "Class, I have a very exciting project to tell you about!"

What would it be? Sharks? Electricity? How sharks use electricity to catch prey?

Nope. It turns out she was talking about *art*.

"Class, this week we will begin working on our biggest art project of the year."

Okay, that sounded fine. Maybe I'd draw a diagram of sharks, or electricity . . .

Ms. Collier continued, "The project is called 'This Is Me,' and it should be an artistic expression of what makes *you* special. I'm giving you a lot of freedom with this project. You can do just about anything you want."

CHRISTINA SOONTORNVAT grew up behind the counter of her parents' Thai restaurant, reading stories. These days she loves to make up her own, especially if they involve magic. Christina also loves science and worked in a science museum for years before pursuing her dream of being an author. She still enjoys cooking up science experiments at home with her two young daughters. You can learn more about Christina and her books on her website at soontornvat.com.

glaciers, Diary!

Princess Lina is the *coolest* girl in school!

scholastic.com